D0574326
B MVFOL
AR PTS: 0.5

David Wojtowycz

# ELEPHANT JOE, Brave Knight!

Moreno Valley Public Library

Random House New York

It was a sunny day at the castle.
Elephant Joe and Zebra Pete
were swimming in the moat.
Suddenly a cry came from the castle.

Help!
Help!
Does someone need
Elephant Joe's help?

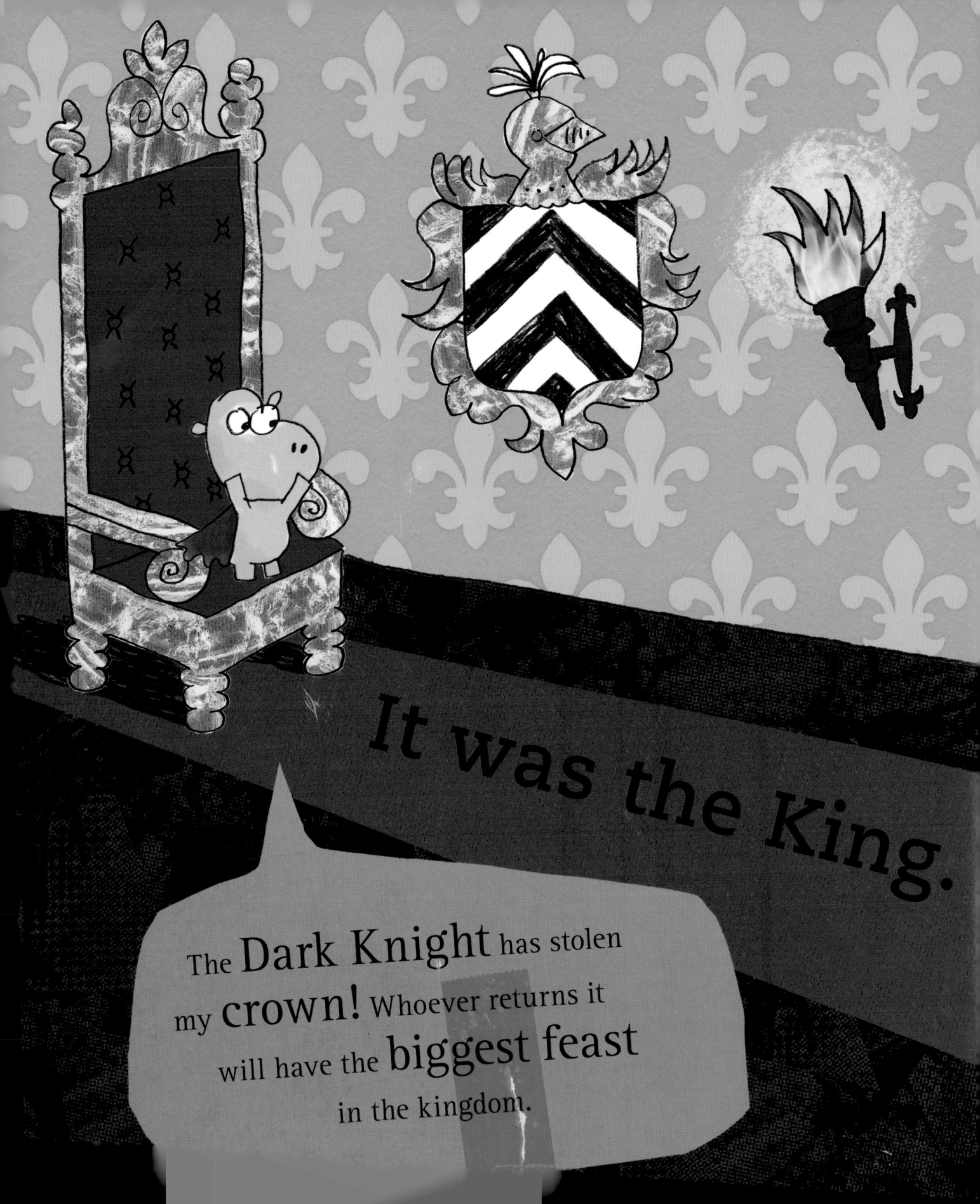
It was the King.
The Dark Knight has stolen my crown! Whoever returns it will have the biggest feast in the kingdom.

Quick!
We need armor!
We need horses!

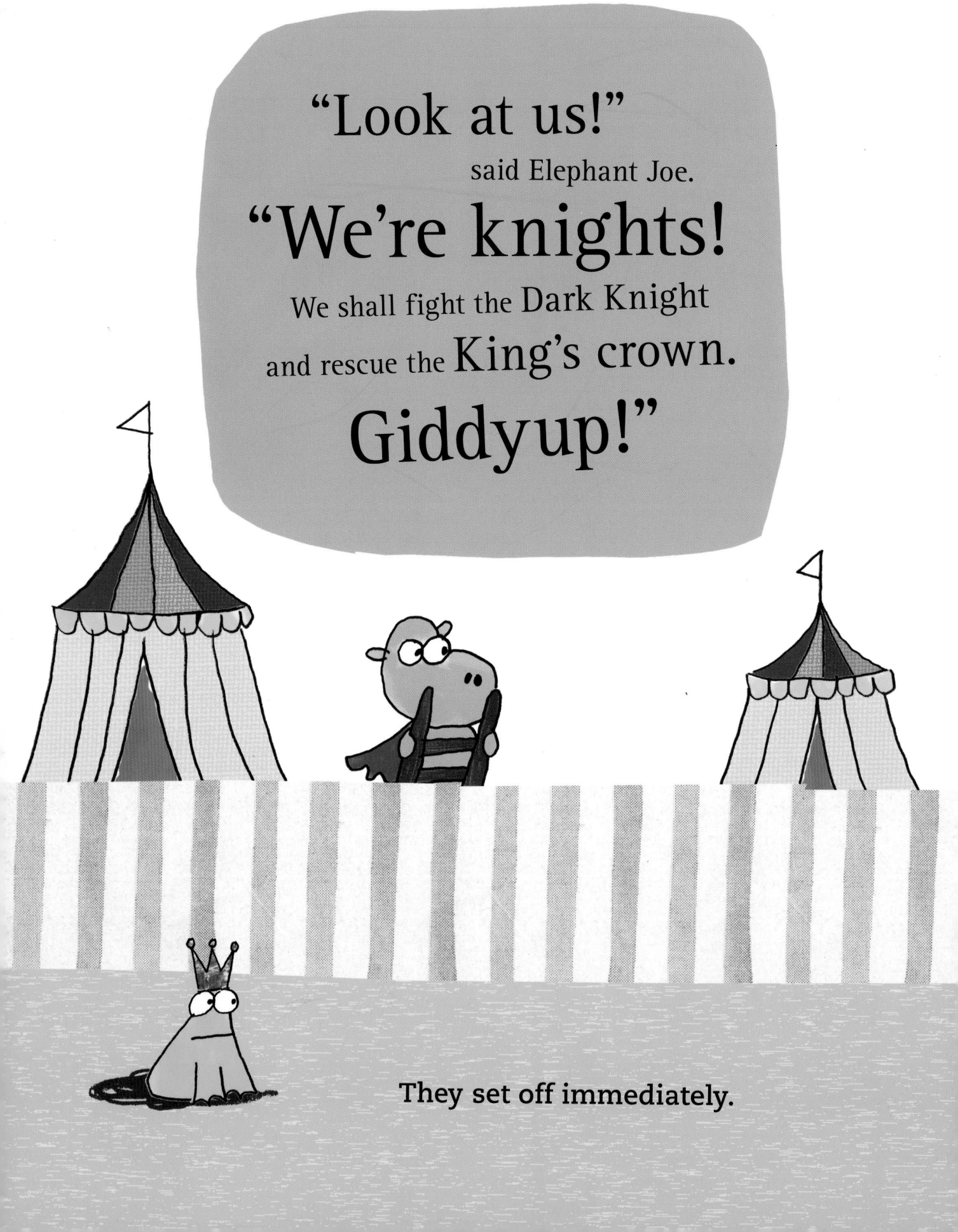
"Look at us!"
said Elephant Joe.
"We're knights!
We shall fight the Dark Knight
and rescue the King's crown.
Giddyup!"
They set off immediately.

Soon they were in the
Enchanted
Forest.

Deep in the forest was the
Dark Knight's tower.
Come on out, Dark Knight.
And bring the King's crown with you!

The Dark Knight's not in. I'm just a damsel in distress.
Fear not, damsel. Elephant Joe will rescue you!

Suddenly there was a terrible **roar**.
Jumping jesters!
We've woken the dreaded dragon!
Back, you beast!
ROAR

The dragon's fire melted
Elephant Joe's sword.

Quick, Zebra Pete!
Joust with him!

The dragon just laughed.
That tickles!
Galloping Galahads!
How will they ever tame this beast?

No one had ever said "please" to the dragon before. He let them past.

We're coming, damsel!
I hope this isn't a trick.

Fair damsel!
You are
rescued!

**But** the damsel was actually . . .

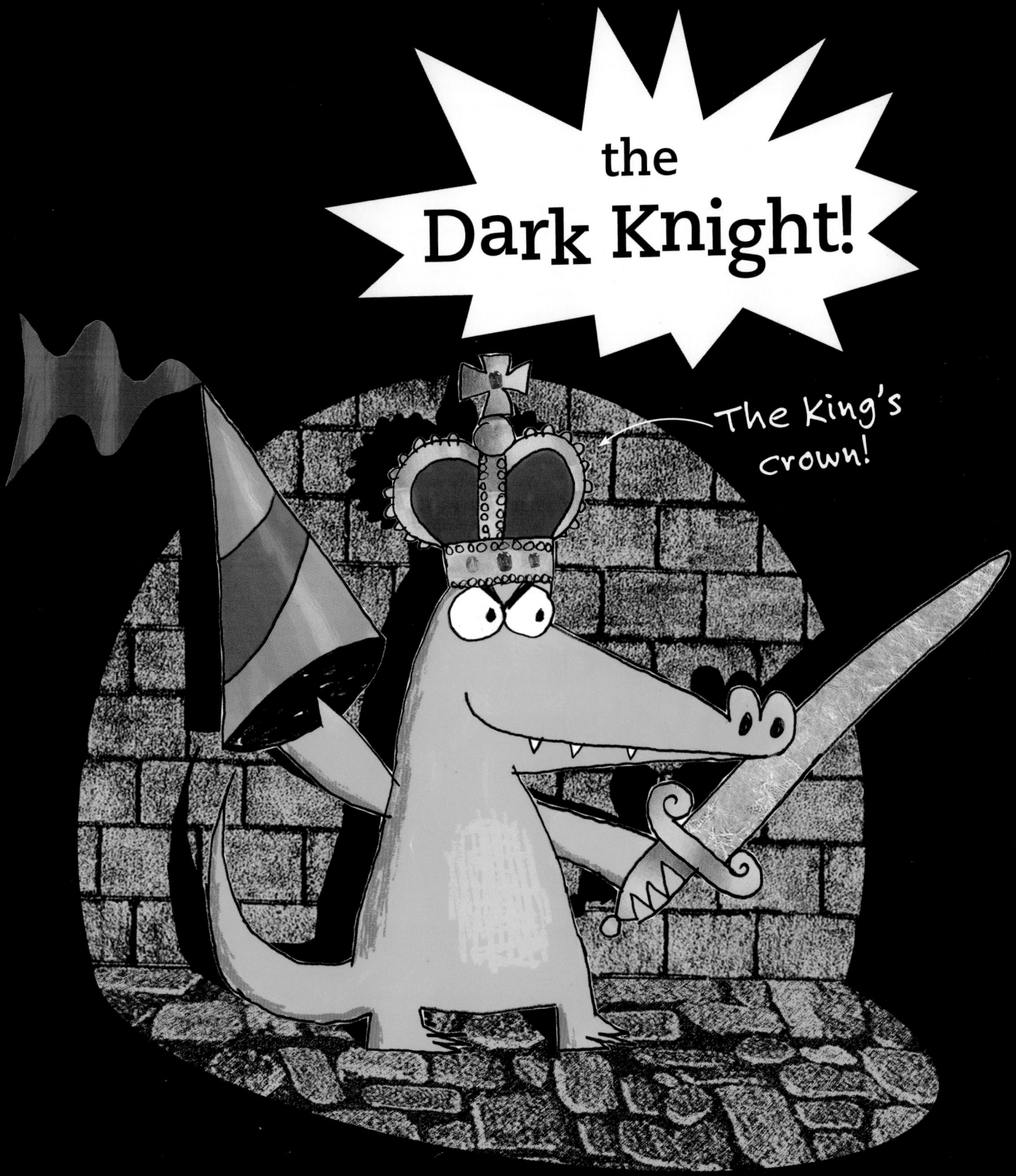

The Dark Knight locked them in her tower.
Then she stole Zebra Pete's horse
and rode away!
Ha-ha!
Now I'm going to be
King of the castle!

Luckily, the dragon had a spare key.
He let them out . . .

. . . and gave them a ride.

There she is! Quick! Head for the castle!
ENCHANTED FOREST

They arrived just in time.

As the drawbridge went up, the horse chucked the Dark Knight into the moat. **Splosh!** went the crown into the water.

Luckily, Elephant Joe was an excellent swimmer.
Stand back!
I shall rescue the King's crown!

Quick as a flash,
he dived into
the moat.

He saved the
crown and
dragged the
Dark Knight
ashore.

The King was very pleased to have his crown back.

"Good idea," said the King. "But first . . ."

". . . let's have our feast!"
Can someone pass the flies, please?

"I like being a knight,"

said Sir Elephant Joe.

To Joe and Zack, from Great-Uncle David

Copyright © 2011 by David Wojtowycz

All rights reserved. Published in the United States by Random House Children's Books, a division of Random House, Inc., New York. Originally published in Great Britain as *Elephant Joe Is a Knight!* by Alison Green Books, an imprint of Scholastic Children's Books, a division of Scholastic Ltd., London, in 2011.

Random House and the colophon are registered trademarks of Random House, Inc.

Visit us on the Web!
www.randomhouse.com/kids

Educators and librarians, for a variety of teaching tools, visit us a
www.randomhouse.com/teachers

Library of Congress Control Number: 2011927722
ISBN 978-0-307-93087-3 (trade)
ISBN 978-0-375-98090-9 (ebook)

MANUFACTURED IN SINGAPORE
10 9 8 7 6 5 4 3 2 1
First American Edition

Random House Children's Books supports the First Amendment and celebrates the right to read.